*Generously donated by*
## Siskiyou/Modoc Child Support Services

*2008*

A STORY ABOUT
UNDERSTANDING DIVORCE

# Two Homes
# for Tyler

BY PAMELA KENNEDY
ILLUSTRATED BY AMY WUMMER

Nashville, Tennessee

ISBN-13: 978-0-8249-5582-3

Published by GPKids
An imprint of Ideals Publications
A Guideposts Company
535 Metroplex Drive, Suite 250
Nashville, Tennessee 37211
www.idealsbooks.com

Color separations by Precision Color Graphics, Franklin, Wisconsin
Printed and bound in Italy by LEGO

Library of Congress CIP data on file


10 9 8 7 6 5 4 3 2 1

Designed by Eve DeGrie

For Vicki, a friend for all seasons.  —P.J.K.

# A Note to Parents
## By Vicki Wiley Lepick

"Honey, Mommy and Daddy still love you very much, but . . ."

Many children have heard these words and felt the pain of them. The words are hard for parents to say and hard for children to hear. But with a little care, the pain can be reduced.

First, do tell your children. Children pick up on signals that something is wrong, and without knowing why, their imaginations can take over. The simple truth is always best.

* Admit that things will change, but reassure the children of both parents' continuing love.
* If possible, share the news with your spouse present. Avoid saying anything that will make your children feel they need to choose sides.
* Let your children respond, and listen to what they have to say. Nothing is too small or too big to discuss.

Every child responds to divorce differently, so don't expect siblings to react in the same way. A child's reaction is often due to how he or she fears life will change. This is a great time for you to remember and convey that God is in control and is there for each of you.

Here are some important ways to take care of yourself and your child:

* Try to keep to your routines. Small children depend on routines for their sense of well-being.
* Be sure to eat well and take care of your health. Make time to exercise together, which can can alleviate stress and anxiety, while providing a time to talk and be together.
* Spend time with family and friends. Don't isolate yourself from others who love you.
* Find support for yourself and your children. There are community and church programs for children of divorce that can be very useful in helping them sort out their feelings.
* Pray with your children in a positive way—asking God to bless your new life.

---

Vicki Wiley Lepick holds a Master of Arts in Theology, with an emphasis on children in crisis, from Fuller Seminary. She is the former Director of Children's Ministries at First Presbyterian Church, Honolulu. Vicki is presently the K-8th grade counselor at St. Andrews Priory, a private girls' school in Honolulu.

**H**i, I'm Tyler. I used to live in a house with Mom and Dad and my puppy, Raggs.

Now Mom and Raggs and I live in our house,

and Dad lives in an apartment with a kitty named Willow.

I used to get up on Saturday morning and jump in bed between Mom and Dad. We'd all laugh and tickle.

Now on Saturdays I cuddle and tickle with Mom in the morning, and Dad comes to get me in the afternoon.

Sometimes Dad and I make popcorn and play games at night when I sleep over.

I used to go fun places like the park and the zoo together with Mom and Dad.

Now Mom and I sometimes play in the park,

and Dad takes me to the zoo or the beach.

I used to take walks together with Mom and Dad.

Now Mom and I ride bikes together,

and Dad helps me practice kicking the soccer ball.

I used to draw pictures to give to Mom and Dad to put on our refrigerator.

Now I sometimes paint a picture for Mom to put on the refrigerator

and make a drawing for Dad to put on his bulletin board.

I used to watch TV at night sitting between Mom and Dad on the couch.

Now sometimes Mom and I watch a TV show together;

and when I'm at Dad's, he and I read stories.

I used to think that I wouldn't see Grammy and Gramps anymore if Mom and Dad got divorced.

Now I know that I can still spend time with Grammy and Gramps.

I used to be afraid that if things changed, I would never be happy again.

Now I know that even though things have changed,

Mom and Dad and I can still be happy.

I used to worry that if Mom and Dad got divorced, they might not love me any more.

Now I know that even though they are divorced,

they both still love me very, very much.

I used to think that it was my fault that Mom and Dad got divorced.

Now I know that it wasn't. Sometimes moms and dads

just decide they cannot be married any more.

I used to think that nobody else knew how I felt about my parents' divorce.

Now I know that there are other kids just like me,

and we can talk about it together if we feel like it.

I used to pray
that God would make
Mom and Dad get
married again.

Now I know that
even though Mom
and Dad aren't
married any more,

God hears and
answers my prayers,
and He loves all of us
very much.

## About the Author

**Pamela Kennedy** lives in Hawaii with her husband and their crooked-tailed, gray-and-white cat, Gilligan. Three days a week, Pamela teaches at a school for girls in Honolulu. When she's not teaching, she writes. She has loved writing stories ever since she was in elementary school. As a teacher and friend, Pam knows that divorce is a subject that touches many families. Through Tyler's story, she hopes to encourage youngsters as well as their parents.

## About the Artist

**Amy Wummer** lives in Reading, Pennsylvania, with her husband Mark, who is also an artist. They have three children: Jesse, Maisie, and Adam. Amy has loved to draw ever since she was a little girl. That's why being a children's book illustrator is the perfect job for her.